A Rookie reader®

Written by Cari Meister
Illustrated by Terry Sirrell

Children's Press®
A Division of Scholastic Inc.
New York • Toronto • London • Auckland • Sydney
Mexico City • New Delhi • Hong Kong
Danbury, Connecticut

Dear Parents/Educators,

Welcome to Rookie Ready to Learn. Each Rookie Reader in this series includes additional age-appropriate Let's Learn Together activity pages that help your young child to be better prepared when starting school. *I Love Trees* offers opportunities for you and your child to talk about the important social/emotional skill of **caring, and how our actions can make a difference**.

Here are early-learning skills you and your child will encounter in the *I Love Trees* Let's Learn Together pages:

• Counting by twos
• Reading a diagram
• Rhyming

We hope you enjoy sharing this delightful, enhanced reading experience with your early learner.

Library of Congress Cataloging-in-Publication Data

Meister, Cari.
   I love trees / written by Cari Meister ; illustrated by Terry Sirrell.
      p. cm. -- (Rookie ready to learn)
   Summary: A child lists some of the many things he loves about trees. Includes suggested learning activities.

   ISBN 978-0-531-26501-7 — ISBN 978-0-531-26733-2 (pbk.)

   [1. Stories in rhyme. 2. Trees--Fiction.] I. Sirrell, Terry, ill. II. Title. III. Series.
   PZ8.3.M5514Im 2011
   [E]--dc22   2010049915

Trees, trees, trees!

3

I love trees!

4

5

Some are big.

6

Some are tiny.

Some are smooth.

Some are spiny.

Some have needles.

Some have leaves.

11

Some have birds.

Some have bees!

Some have apples.

Some have pears.

Some have owls.

Some have bears!

Trees, trees, trees!
I love trees!

They make boats.

They make stables.

They make paper.

They make tables.

They make toys.
They make beds.

They make chairs.

They make sleds.

They make tools.

They make swings.

They make drums.

They make lots of things!

Trees, trees, trees!
I love trees.

Congratulations!

You just finished reading *I Love Trees* and learned many reasons why it is important to care for trees and the earth.

About the Author
Cari Meister lives on a small farm in Minnesota with her husband and sons. She is the author of more than twenty books for children.

About the Illustrator
Cartoonist and illustrator Terry Sirrell has been drawing since 1983. His work can be seen everywhere from the backs of cereal boxes to magazines and books.

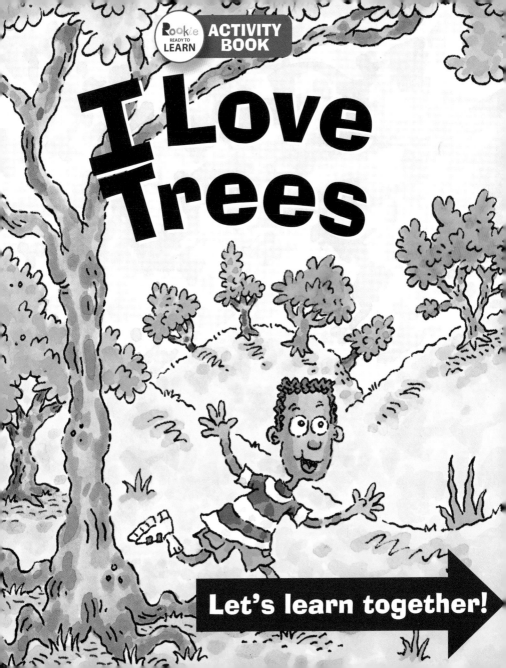

Planting a Tree

(Sing this song to the tune
of "This Is the Way.")

This is the way we plant a tree,
plant a tree, plant a tree.

This is the way we plant a tree,
so early in the morning.

(Repeat with these verses:)

This is the way we plant the seeds…

This is the way the rain waters
the seeds…

This is the way the sun feeds
the seeds…

This is the way the apples grow…

This is the way we pick the apples…

This is the way we eat the apples…

PARENT TIP: Learning about our environment and playing outdoors are important for your child's social/emotional and academic development. Being outdoors helps to teach children about the world around them and gives them an appreciation for nature, encouraging them to become stewards of our earth. Additionally, playing outdoors provides children with opportunities for physical activity.

Bees Like Trees

The boy learned a lot about trees. He learned that some have pears. He learned that some have bears. What else did he learn? Help the boy match words that rhyme.

Look at each picture. Say its name. Then point to a picture that shows what rhymes with it.

bed   tree   pear

bee   sled   bear

PARENT TIP: Rhyming games help children learn to listen carefully to every sound in a word. They help develop a skill known as *phonological awareness*. Phonological awareness is the idea that words are made up of separate sounds. Other ways to build this skill are through singing rhyming songs, reading rhyme books, and making up silly rhymes.

We Love Trees

The boy in the story loves trees.

He loves that trees are homes for many animals and that fruit grows on some trees. Look closely at this picture. How many of each animal do you count? How many apples? How many pine trees? When you count each group of things in the boxes, you will have counted by twos.

PARENT TIP: You may want to begin by counting by ones, such as 1, 2, 3, 4, and so on. Then point out to your child that there is another way to count. Show your child how to count by twos, such as 2, 4, 6, 8, 10. Counting by twos helps children later understand multiplication.

Planting a Tree

(Sing this song to the tune of "Head, Shoulders, Knees, and Toes.")

Leaves, branches, trunk, and roots.
(Wiggle fingers and hands for leaves; stretch arms out for branches.)

Trunk and roots.
(Touch body for the trunk and touch feet for the roots.)

Leaves, branches, trunk, and roots.

Trunk and roots.

Trees are important to you and to me.

Leaves, branches, trunk, and roots.

Trunk and roots!

PARENT TIP: Relating parts of a tree to parts of our bodies helps children come to understand that trees are living things and that each part plays an important role in the tree's growth and life. The leaves make food for the tree. The leaves and stems are connected to the branches, and the branches are connected to the trunk. The trunk is where water moves up to the leaves and the food moves down to the roots. The roots help the tree stand tall and bring water and nutrients to the tree.

branches

leaves

trunk

roots

Plant Care

Plants need our care. See what happens if we do not provide plants with the sunlight that they need.

YOU WILL NEED: **Black construction paper**

A healthy house plant  **Paper clips**

1

Cut two pieces of construction paper that are big enough to cover a leaf. Cover the leaf, top and bottom, and fasten with paper clips.

2

Leave the plant in the sunlight. Water the plant, if needed. Wait a week. Then remove the construction paper. Observe what happened to the leaf with no sunlight.

PARENT TIP: Most children want to do their part to take care of the earth. Include your child in a recycling plan for your home. He can assist with placing bottles, cans, and newspapers in the proper receptacles. You can remind your child that this positive action helps the earth and all of its inhabitants.

I Love Trees Word List (34 Words)

apples	have	pears	tiny
are	I	sleds	tools
bears	leaves	smooth	toys
beds	lots	some	trees
bees	love	spiny	
big	make	stables	
birds	needles	swings	
boats	of	tables	
chairs	owls	they	
drums	paper	things	

PARENT TIP: Point out the words on this list that your child already rhymed: *bed, tree,* and *pear.* Write those words in three columns on a sheet of paper. Think of more words that rhyme with those words and write them in the columns.